Silly Monsters
ABC

Silly Monsters ABC

Gerald Hawksley

A is for the amblemoose,
who ambles aimlessly.

B is for the buzzlesnout,
who buzzes like a bee.

Cc is for the crococodo,
who crunches carrot cake.

D is for the drooling dampwottle,
who dribbles by the lake.

enormous eye

ear

Ee

egg

eleflopple

E is for the eleflopple,
who has one enormous eye.

F is for the funny little furry floodlefly.

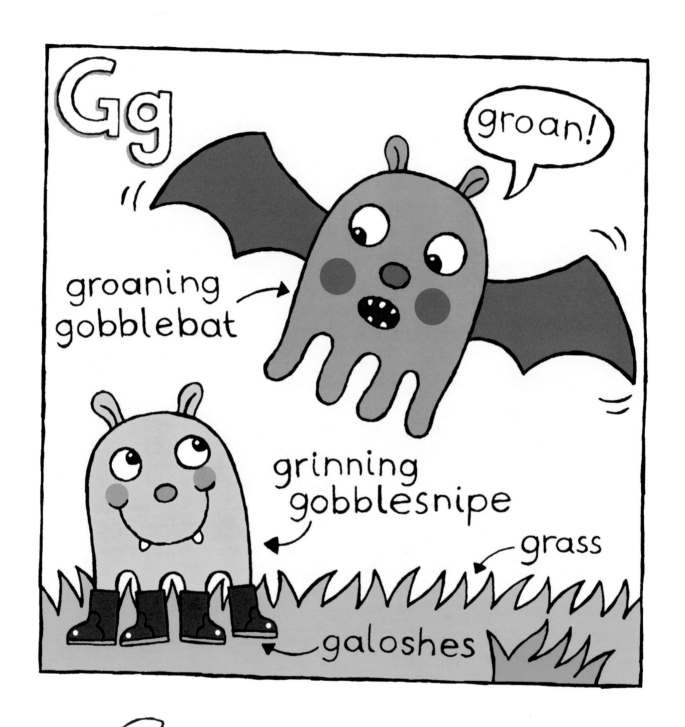

G is for the gobblesnipe,
and the gobblebat.

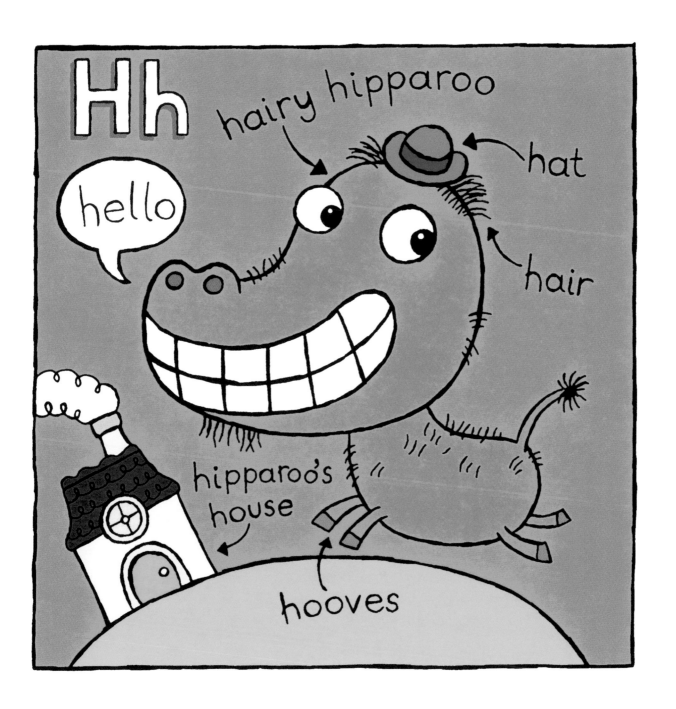

H is for the hairy hipparoo,
who likes to wear a hat.

I is for the inkfish,
who bathes in ink indoors.

J is for the jumbug,
who has enormous jaws.

kennel

kipperdog

Kk

kitten

kedgeree

K is for the kindly kipperdog.

L is for the logmonster,
who looks just like a log.

M is for the mouldy moop,
who menaces mild-mannered mice.

N is for the nasty nonk,
who's never very nice.

O is for the oddly named ooblong.

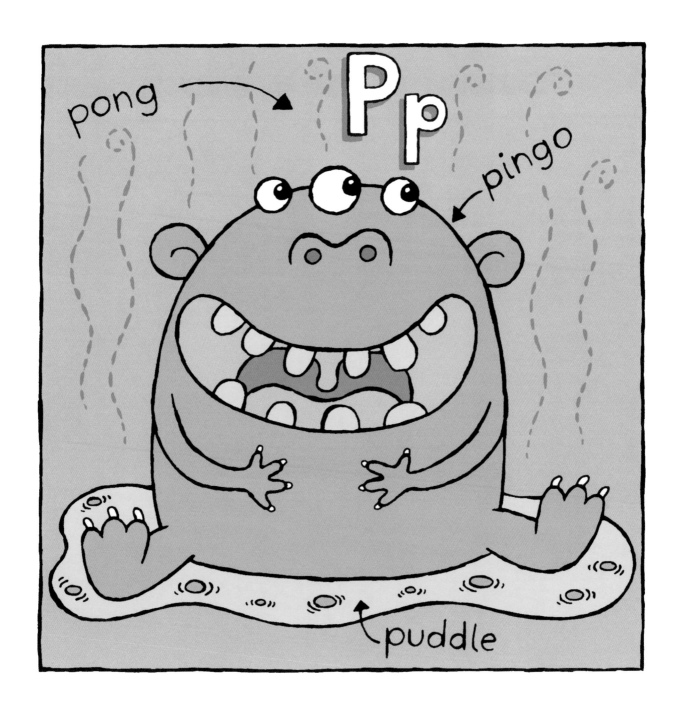

P is for the pingo,
who makes a putrid pong.

Q is for the queeple,
who sits on a quilt and quivers.

R is for the ratatoon,
who resides in rural rivers.

S is for the spotty socksniffer,
who sniffs at socks with spots.

T is for the tea-toad,
who hides in cracked teapots.

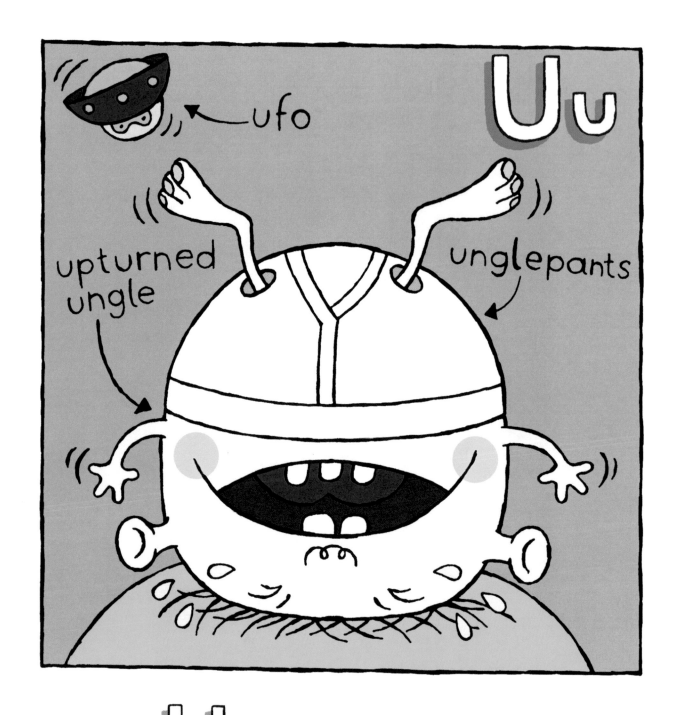

U is for the ungle,
who upturns when upset.

V is for the veryworm,
who's visiting the vet.

W is for the wollery,
who is wonderful and wise.

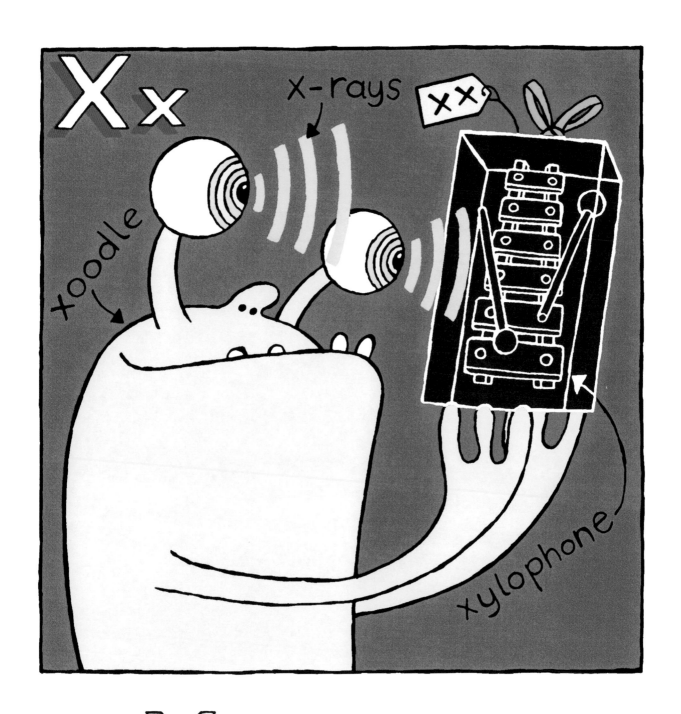

X is for the xoodle,
who has extraordinary x-ray eyes.

Y is for the yawning yobbler.
What a sleepyhead!

and **Z** is for the zebozoo,
who is sleeping in his bed!

ZZZZZZZZ
ZZ   ZZ
Z   ZZZZZZZ   Z
Z   ZZ   ZZ   Z
Z   ZZ   Z   Z
Z   Z   The   Z   Z
Z   z   End   Z   Z
Z   z z   N   Z
Z   z z   z   Z
Z   z z z   z z   Z
Z   z z z z z z z   N
Z   z z z z z z z   Z
ZZ   z Z
Z ZZ   ZZ Z
Z   ZZ   ZZ   Z
Z   ZZZZZZ   Z
ZZ   ZZ
ZZ   ZZ
ZZZZZZ

zzzzzZZZZZZ

Made in the USA
Charleston, SC
16 October 2013